THE LAST DAYS OF POMPEII

EDWARD BULWER-LYTTON

In 79 A.D., the city of Pompeii was a gay summer retreat. Its people were carefree and self-indulgent. They had the Bay of Naples on one side, and the volcano, Mount Vesuvius, on the other.

One ne summer day, two rich young men were sauntering through the streets of Pompeii.

Talk to me no more of Rome, Clodius. Pleasure is too stately and ponderous there. Here we have luxury without pomp.

Therefore, Glaucus, you chose your summer retreat here?

Yes. The Romans do everything so heavily, even to the way they mimic my Athenian ancestors.

Their heir steps were arrested by a crowd gathered round a young girl with a flower basket on her right arm and a small instrument of music in her left hand. She was blind.

It is my poor Thessalian.* I have not seen her since my return to Pompeii.

* a native of Thessaly, a region of ancient Greece

Pressing ressing through the crowd, Glaucus dropped a handful of small coins in her basket.

I must have yon bunch of violets, sweet Nydia.

The he girl started at his voice, while the blood rushed violently to neck, cheek and temples.

Glaucus is returned!

Yes, child. My garden wants your care as before. You will visit it, I trust, tomorrow.

Nydia smiled joyously. Glaucus turned gaily from the crowd.

She interests me, the poor slave. Besides, she is of Thessaly.

The witches' country.

True, but for my part I find every woman a witch.

Lo, here comes one of the handsomest in Pompeii, the rich Julia.

A young lady attended by two female slaves approached them.

Has Glaucus forgotten his friends of the last year?

Beautiful Julia! Never one so fair!

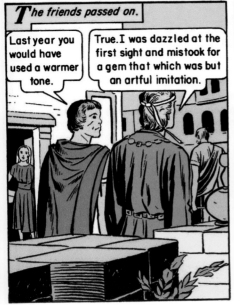

The friends passed on.

Last year you would have used a warmer tone.

True. I was dazzled at the first sight and mistook for a gem that which was but an artful imitation.

They were now in a street less crowded than the rest, at the end of which they beheld the broad and lovely sea.

They bent their steps toward the beach and, seated on a small crag, inhaled the cooling breeze.

Tell me, Clodius, hast thou ever been in love?

Very often. Art thou?

No, but I could be, were I to see the object. Several months ago I was sojourning at Neapolis.* One day I entered the Temple of Minerva.

*Naples.

"The temple was empty, but suddenly I heard a deep sigh. I turned and behind me was a female. When our eyes met, methought a celestial ray shot from those orbs into my soul.

"Never have I seen a mortal face more exquisitely moulded. We made our offerings together and silently left the temple. I was about to ask her where she dwelt when a youth took her hand, the crowd separated us, and I saw her no more."

I instituted inquiries but could discover naught of her. Hoping to lose in gaiety all remembrance of that beautiful apparition, I hastened to plunge myself midst the luxuries of Pompeii.

As Clodius was about to reply, Arbaces, an Egyptian, approached them.

The scene must, indeed, be beautiful which draws the gay Clodius and Glaucus from the crowded city.

Is nature ordinarily so unattractive?

To the dissipated, yes.

After all, you do right to enjoy the hour while it smiles for you. And we, O Glaucus, strangers in the land and far from our fathers' ashes, what is there left for us but pleasure or regret?

Arbaces gathered his robe around him and slowly swept away.

I breathe more freely. Yon gliding shadow is enough to sour the richest grape.

The young men returned to the city. That night Glaucus entertained a group of his friends. Clodius proposed a toast.

Companions, I give you the beautiful Ione!

The name is Greek. I drink the health with delight, but who is Ione?

She has but lately come to Pompeii. Her beauty is dazzling. Her house is perfect. She is rich. She has all Pompeii at her feet, yet she will not marry.

A miracle! Can we not see her?

I will take you there this evening.

Glaucus and Clodius adjourned to the house of the fair lady. They found Ione already surrounded by adoring and applauding guests.

At that moment the group, dividing on either side of Ione, gave to Glaucus' view that bright beauty which for months had shone down upon the waters of his memory.

It is the same woman I saw in the Temple of Minerva at Neapolis!

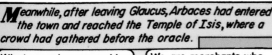

Meanwhile, after leaving Glaucus, Arbaces had entered the town and reached the Temple of Isis, where a crowd had gathered before the oracle.

What occasion assembles you before the altars of Isis?

We are merchants who seek to know the fate of our vessels, which sail tomorrow.

A dead silence fell over the crowd as a hollow voice came from the oracle.

On the brow of the future the dangers lower,
But blest are your barks in the fearful hour.

The crowd dispersed happily, but the Egyptian lingered until one of the priests appeared.

Calenus, you have improved the voice of the statue much by attending to my suggestion; and your verses are excellent. Always prophesy good fortune, unless there is an absolute impossibility of its fulfillment.

The two men went to one of the small chambers near the gate and seated themselves.

You know that in Neapolis I encountered Ione and Apaecides, brother and sister, children of Athenians. The death of their parents, who knew and esteemed me, constituted me their guardian. The youth, docile and mild, I taught the solemn faith of Isis.

Our speaking statues and secret staircases dismay and revolt him. He pines; he refuses to share our ceremonies.

This is what I feared. I must find him: I must continue my lessons. I will thus fulfill my object with Apaecides and carry on my design for Ione. I intend her for my queen, my bride.

I hear from a thousand lips that she is a second Helen.

Yes, she has a beauty that Greece itself never excelled. And she has a genius--keen, dazzling, bold. This is the nature I have sought all my life in woman, and never found till now. Ione must be mine!

Hast thou no fear of rivals?

None. Her Greek soul despises the barbarian Romans. But it is time for me to begin my operations on her fancies and her heart. I will invite her to my house and under veil of the mysteries of religion, I will open to her the secrets of love.

The next morning, Glaucus sought the house of Ione. In passing his threshold, he encountered the blind flower girl tending his flowers.

Poor Nydia, thine is a hard doom. Thou seest not the earth, nor the sun, nor the stars. Above all, thou canst not behold Ione.

Glaucus found Ione at home. They spoke of Greece, a theme on which Ione loved to listen.

From that time they daily saw each other. In the evening, they made excursions on the placid sea. Their talk turned to Ione's brother.

He is a priest of Isis. Arbaces kindled in him this pious desire.

So young, and that priesthood so severe.

I wish that Apaecides had not been so hasty. Perhaps, like all who expect too much, he is revolted too easily.

I know Arbaces. His gloomy brow and icy smiles seem to me to sadden the very sun.

Perhaps it is only the exhaustion of past sufferings, as yonder Vesuvius, now dark and tranquil, once nursed fires now forever quenched.

One day, Arbaces discovered Glaucus at Ione's house. When Glaucus was gone...

May I speak as a friend, without reserve and without offence?

I beseech you to do so.

This young Glaucus only yesterday boasted openly in the public baths of your love. He said it amused him to take advantage of you. He laughed when Clodius asked him if he loved you enough for marriage.

Impossible!

Nay, the story has circulated through the town. I own it vexed me to hear your name thus lightly pitched from lip to lip!

Ione sank back, her face white. Arbaces turned the conversation to other things.

I have seen your brother Apaecides. For some time he has been troubled of spirit, but I have calmed his mind. They who trust themselves to Arbaces never repent of it.

Fair Ione, I value you beyond all others. You have never seen the interior of my home; it may amuse you to do so. Devote then, to me, one of these bright summer evenings.

A date was fixed for the visit, and the Egyptian departed. Ione now refused to see any suitors. Glaucus was excluded with the rest. One day, he went with some friends to the house where the gladiators congregated.

Holla, my brave fellows! We have come to see which of you to bet upon.

What fine animals!

It is a pity they are not warriors.

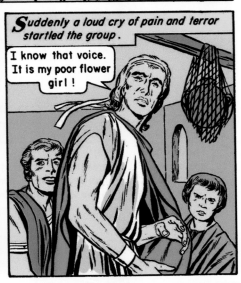

Suddenly a loud cry of pain and terror startled the group.

I know that voice. It is my poor flower girl!

Glaucus darted at once into the room whence the cry rose and beheld Nydia writhing in the grasp of her mistress, the owner of the house.

How dare you use thus a girl?

She is to sing at a banquet given by one who pays liberally, and she will not.

I will go no more to that unholy place.

Glaucus seated himself on one of the rude chairs and held Nydia on his knees.

Fear not, sweet Nydia.

Oh, do not forsake me!

This is your slave; she sings well, she is accustomed to the care of flowers. I wish to make a present of such a slave to a lady. Will you sell her to me?

The girl is worth twelve sestertia.

You shall have twenty.

The sale was concluded.

Then I am to go with you? O happiness!

Pretty one, yes. Thy hardest task henceforth shall be to sing thy hymns to the loveliest lady in Pompeii.

The girl sprang from his clasp. A change came over her whole face.

I thought I was to go to your house.

And so thou shalt, for the present. Come, we lose time.

Three days passed. Then...

Nydia, my child, thou hast now recovered somewhat from the hateful recollections of thy former state. I am about to pray at thine hands a boon.

Hast thou ever heard the name of Ione? I am about to send thee to her. Take her the fairest flowers thou canst pluck, and give her, also, this letter.

Nydia burst into tears.

My child, she is gentle and kind. She will love thy simple graces. Wilt thou not do for me this kindness?

If I can serve thee, command.

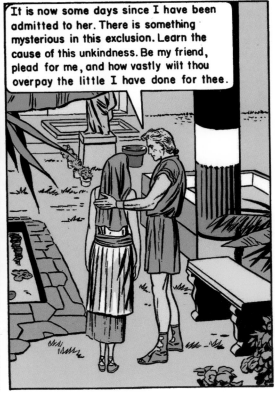

It is now some days since I have been admitted to her. There is something mysterious in this exclusion. Learn the cause of this unkindness. Be my friend, plead for me, and how vastly wilt thou overpay the little I have done for thee.

Nydia went to Ione's house and was admitted to her chamber.

I come from Glaucus. This letter will explain why he sent me.

Ione gazed upon the young slave in compassion. Then, retiring a little from her, she opened and read the letter.

"For five days have I been banished from thy presence. Do I offend thee? Am I too bold? Ione, there is something kindred between us, and our eyes acknowledge it. Deign to see me, to listen to me."

"Canst thou confound me with the common flatterers that flock around thee? Have they slandered me to thee, Ione? Thou wilt not believe them. Accept my homage and my vows. Farewell."

Ione's heart smote her. Tears rolled down her cheeks. She wrote an answer.

Come to me tomorrow, Glaucus. I may have been unjust to thee, but I will tell thee the fault that has been imputed to thy charge. Fear not henceforth.

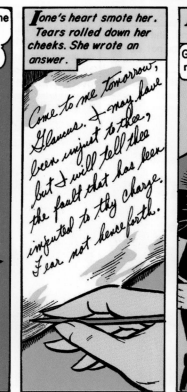

Ione bent down and kissed Nydia.

Go, my child, take him this letter. But return again. Thou shalt be to me a friend.

Nydia delivered the answer to Glaucus. It was evening when Nydia once more gained the house of Ione, who had long left it.

Whither hath she gone?

To the house of Arbaces, the Egyptian.

Impossible! Has she often visited him before?

Never till now.

Nydia left the house.

She does not dream of the dangers into which she has plunged. It was to Arbaces' banquets I would not go. Shall I save her? Yes, for I love Glaucus better than myself.

When she arrived at the house of Glaucus, she learnt that he had gone out and none knew whither.

Knowest thou if Ione has any relative, any intimate friend at Pompeii?

Everyone in Pompeii knows Ione has a brother, Apaecides, who has been so foolish as to become a priest of Isis.

Nydia hastened to the neighbouring Temple of Isis, where a slave pointed out the one she sought.

Apaecides, Ione is in the halls of Arbaces. Thou knowest the peril. I will lead thee to the private door.

On the way, they encountered Glaucus. A few words sufficed to make him their companion. Meanwhile, Ione had entered the spacious hall of the Egyptian and had been met by Arbaces in festive robes.

Beautiful Ione, it is thou who hath eclipsed the day. Thine eyes light up the hall.

You must not talk to me thus. It was you who taught me to disdain adulation.

He led her through various chambers, which seemed to contain the treasures of the world. Suddenly, as they stood in one hall, the Egyptian clapped his hands and a banquet rose from the floor.

When the feast was over, Arbaces led Ione to another room and knelt at her feet.

Thou art destined to be the bride of Arbaces. Oh, Ione! I adore thee! I have sought the world around and found none like thee. Thou art my queen, my goddess. Be my bride!

Ione was confused, astonished.

Rise, Arbaces. You have been my guardian, my friend. Think not I am not honoured by this homage; but I love another.

His name is Glaucus! Thou shalt go to thy tomb rather than to his arms. Thou art mine, only mine!

He caught Ione in his arms. She tore herself from him. He seized her — again she broke away and fell with a loud shriek at the base of a column.

Arbaces had once more darted upon his prey when the curtain was rudely torn aside. The Egyptian beheld the flashing eyes of Glaucus and the pale but menacing countenance of Apaecides.

Ah, what Fury hath sent ye hither?

Glaucus closed at once with the Egyptian. Both antagonists were locked in each other's grasp, the hand of each seeking the throat of the other.

At last, they drew back for breath — Arbaces leaning against a column which supported the head of the Egyptian goddess, Isis. Arbaces clasped the column and raised his eyes toward the sacred image.

O ancient goddess, protect thy chosen.

As he spoke, the still features of the goddess seemed suddenly to glow with life. Through the black marble flushed a crimson hue. The eyes became like balls of fire.

Glaucus stood dismayed, aghast. Arbaces gave him not breathing time to recover his stupor, but sprang upon him. The Greek lost his footing. He fell.

Apaecides rushed forward. His knife gleamed in the air. But the Egyptian, with one sweeping blow, stretched him to the earth. Then Arbaces brandished the knife over Glaucus.

At that awful instant the floor shook under them. The dread demon of the earthquake roused itself from the sleep of years. The column trembled. The head of the goddess fell from its pedestal and struck the Egyptian like the blow of death.

Glaucus staggered to his feet. He assisted Apaecides to rise and, taking up Ione, fled from the unhallowed spot.

In the days following, Glaucus and Ione talked only of their love. Of Arbaces, they heard that he recovered slowly from the shock he had sustained. One evening, as Nydia walked alone, she was interrupted by a female voice.

Blind flower girl, dost thou not know my voice? I am Julia, the daughter of Diomed, the wealthy. Come, I have much to ask of thee.

Nydia followed Julia to her house.

You serve Ione. Does Glaucus find her handsome?

I should think so, since they are soon to be wedded.

Julia, turning pale, started from her couch. She remained a long time silent. Then...

They tell me thou art a Thessalian. Thessaly is the land of magic and witches, of talismans and love philtres. Knowest thou any love charms?

I? No, assuredly not. But Julia has money and youth and loveliness. Are they not love charms enough?

To all but one person in the world.

And that one person?

Is not Glaucus.

Nydia drew her breath more freely.

But tell me, hast thou ever heard of any Eastern magician in this city who possesses the art of which thou art ignorant?

What Pompeian has not heard of Arbaces?

May I visit him?

It is an evil mansion, but at daylight and in his present state, thou hast assuredly the less to fear.

Julia sought an audience with Arbaces that very day.

Pardon me that I rise with pain. I am still suffering from a recent illness.

Do not disturb thyself, and forgive an unfortunate female who seeks advice in unhappy love.

I have left the witchery of philtres to those who trade in such knowledge. Yet I will give thee advice if thou wilt be candid with me. Wilt thou confide in me the name of thy love?

He is of Athens.

Ha, there is but one Athenian, young and noble, in Pompeii. Can it be Glaucus?

So indeed they call him.

The Egyptian sank back, muttering to himself of revenge.

Listen to me. At the base of Vesuvius dwells a powerful witch. Her art can bring thy lover to thy feet.

A meeting was arranged for the next evening, and Julia departed. Arbaces called for a litter and set out for the witch's cave.

A superior in thine art salutes thee. Hear me, then, and obey.

There cometh to thee by tomorrow's starlight a vain maiden, seeking a love charm. Instead of thy philtres, give the maiden one of thy most powerful poisons.

But I shall surely be detected. The dead ever find avengers. Instead, I will give one that shall sear and blast the brain, make him who quaffs it an abject, raving thing.

How much more exquisite than death!

Arbaces passed into the moonlit air and hastened down the mountain. The hag bent to look into a deep, irregular fissure in the earth from whence came a distant grating noise and streaks of red light.

Strange! What can it portend?

The next evening, the witch gave the philtre to Julia. Nydia waited for Julia's return.

Oh, such a scene, such fearful incantations! But I have obtained the potion. My rival shall be suddenly indifferent to his eye and I, I alone, the idol of Glaucus!

Glaucus!

Aye, I told thee, girl, at first, that it was not the Athenian. But I see now that I may trust thee wholly. It is the beautiful Greek.

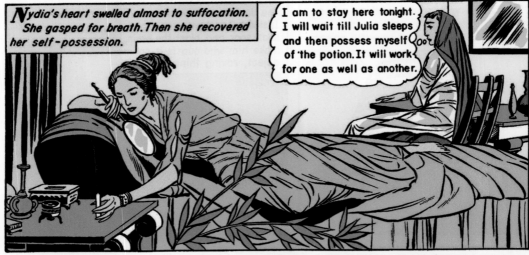

Nydia's heart swelled almost to suffocation. She gasped for breath. Then she recovered her self-possession.

I am to stay here tonight. I will wait till Julia sleeps and then possess myself of the potion. It will work for one as well as another.

They retired to their couches, and Julia soon slept. Nydia rose gently, emptied a perfume bottle, poured the contents of the phial into it, then refilled the phial with water which the potion so resembled.

In the morning, she placed the treasure in her tunic and hastened to quit the house.

Glaucus, my fate is in thy smile; and thy fate is in these hands.

One day, Julia's father held a banquet. Glaucus was among the guests. Julia, having put what she thought was the potion in a cup, contrived to draw him apart.

You have drunk many toasts with my father. Drink one now with me. Health and fortune to your bride!

She presented the cup to Glaucus. He drained the whole contents and began to converse in the same tone as before.

The witch said the effect might not be immediate. But tomorrow, alas for Glaucus!

Glaucus soon left. When he arrived at his own home, he found Nydia seated under the portico of his garden.

Ho, my child, wait you for me? It has been warm. I long for some cooling drink.

I will prepare one for you myself.

She withdrew for a few minutes and returned with a cup containing the potion. He raised it to his lips and had drained about a fourth of its contents when his eye, suddenly glancing at Nydia, was struck by her strange expression.

He rose to approach her. A sudden pang shot coldly to his heart and was followed by wild, confused sensations at the brain. He clapped his hands, he bounded aloft. Incoherent words gushed from his lips. Nydia fell on the ground and embraced his knees.

Glaucus! Do you not know me? Rave not so wildly.

Who calls? Ione, it is she! They have borne her off. We will save her. I come! I come!

Nydia fell insensible as Glaucus rushed down the starlit street.

He passed the more populous streets and entered the lonely grove of Cybele. There, it chanced, Arbaces had just encountered Apaecides.

Villain, thou hast recovered then from the jaws of the grave? But think not to weave around me thy guilty meshes. I am armed against thee!

Hush! I have repented bitterly of my madness. I ask thy sister in marriage.

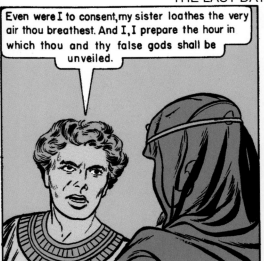

Several citizens came thronging to the place.

Lift up the corpse, and guard well the murderer.

Glaucus! Is it even credible?

A centurion* thrust himself into the gathering crowd.

Who accuses the murderer?

I. Passing through the grove, I beheld the Greek and the priest in earnest conversation. I was struck by the violent gestures of the first. Suddenly, I saw him raise his stilus. I darted forward -- too late to arrest the blow.

*captain in the Roman army

I struck the murderer to the ground. He fell without a struggle, which makes me suspect he was not altogether in his senses.

Oh, mercy -- I burn! Marrow and brain, I burn.

He raves, and in his delirium he has struck the priest. We must take him to the praetor*.

*judge

As Arbaces turned to go, he met the eyes of the priest Calenus. There was something significant and sinister in the glance.

Could he have witnessed the deed?

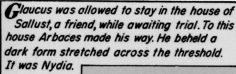

Glaucus was allowed to stay in the house of Sallust, a friend, while awaiting trial. To this house Arbaces made his way. He beheld a dark form stretched across the threshold. It was Nydia.

Oh, save him! He is not guilty. It is I! Oh, heal him.

Hush. What must be, must

The Egyptian was taken to Glaucus, who had recovered his senses.

I can save thee. I can prove thou wert bereaved of sense. Only sign this paper acknowledging the crime.

I, the murderer of Ione's brother? Let me rather perish a thousand times.

Beware! Thy confession or the amphitheatre and the lion's maw! It is the season for the games, and the people seek a victim.

Who will debase his name to save his life? Go. My eyes loathe the sight of thee.

The Egyptian left the chamber. In the street, Nydia once more started from her long watch. Arbaces bade her follow him.

I must secure this girl lest she give evidence of the philtre. As to the vain Julia, she will not betray herself.

Nydia followed the Egyptian to his house.

Daughter, thou must rest here. It is not meet for thee to wander along the streets. Wait here patiently for some days and Glaucus will be restored.

He hastened from the room, drew the bolt across the door, and consigned the care of his prisoner to a slave.

I must also secure Ione. She must not interest herself in the trial, for she might cast doubt on me.

He ordered a covered litter and set out early the next morning to intercept Ione as she took her way homeward from the funeral of her brother.

Now to Glaucus. Let me soothe, tend, cheer him. And if they sentence him to exile or death, let me share the sentence with him.

She came suddenly upon a small knot of men standing beside a covered litter. Arbaces stepped from the midst of them.

Fair Ione, my ward. The praetor hath wisely confined thee to the care of thy lawful guardian.

Begone! It is thou that hast slain my brother.

Thy sorrows unstring thy reason, Ione. Approach, slaves. Place her in the litter.

The slaves obeyed, and the unfortunate Ione was borne to another chamber in Arbaces' house. Meanwhile, Nydia grew impatient and called aloud. Sosia, the slave in attendance, opened the door.

Ho, girl! Thinkest thou we are dying of silence here?

Where is thy master? And wherefore am I caged here? Let me go forth.

Arbaces has ordered thee to be caged, and caged thou art.

What can Arbaces want with so poor a thing as I am?

That I know not. But if thou wantest a companion, I am willing to talk to thee. Thou art Thessalian -- knowest thou not some pretty trick of telling fortunes, as most of thy race do?

Tush, slave, hold thy peace, or if thou wilt speak, what hast thou heard of Glaucus?

If he be found guilty, the lion will be his executioner.

Nydia leaped up as if an arrow had entered her heart.

Tell me thou jestest. Speak, speak!

It may not be as bad as I say. But Arbaces is his accuser, and the people desire a victim for the arena.

When his household cares obliged the slave to leave, Nydia began to collect her thoughts.

To escape, I must work upon my keeper. I remember his superstitious query as to my Thessalian art.

When the slave came again...

You would have answers to your future? Then come here three hours after twilight and thou shalt learn all, according to the Thessalian lore my mother taught me.

But first be sure that thou leavest the garden gate somewhat open, so that the demon I shall consult may feel himself invited to enter therein: Forget it not. All rests upon that.

Later that evening, the anxious slave stole into the blind girl's chamber.

Well, Sosia, art thou prepared? Hast thou left the garden gate open?

Yes.

That's well. Now, leave this door just ajar. Then seat thyself.

The slave obeyed, and Nydia began to chant. Then...

The spectre is certainly coming. I feel him running along my hair. Give me thy napkin, and let me fold up thy face and eyes.

Address to the spectre whatever question thou wouldst ask him.

O Spirit! Shall I be able to purchase my freedom next year?

The slave continued to talk to the spirit without obtaining an answer. Finally, in a rage, he managed to extricate his head from the napkin.

What ho! The lamp is gone. Ah, traitress, thou art gone too. But I'll catch thee. Thou shalt smart for this!

The slave groped his way to the door. It was bolted from without. He was a prisoner instead of Nydia.

I dare not call out lest Arbaces overhear me. But tomorrow, when the slaves are at work, I can make myself heard. Then I can go forth and seek her and bring her back before Arbaces knows a word of the matter.

Meanwhile, Nydia was about to proceed toward the garden gate when she heard behind her the voices of Arbaces and the priest Calenus. She hastily descended some narrow stairs and felt herself in unknown ground.

The air is damp and chill. I must be among the cellars of the mansion.

Presently, Calenus and Arbaces drew near.

The gay Glaucus will be lodged tomorrow in apartments not much drier than this.

And to think a word of thine could save him and consign Arbaces to his doom.

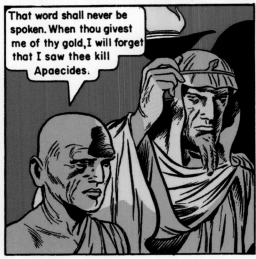

That word shall never be spoken. When thou givest me of thy gold, I will forget that I saw thee kill Apaecides.

Arbaces now unlocked a small door set in the wall.

Enter, my friend, while I hold the lamp on high that thou mayest glut thine eyes on the yellow heaps.

Scarcely had Calenus crossed the threshold when the strong hand of Arbaces plunged him forward and closed the door.

Starve, wretch! Farewell!

The remorseless Egyptian departed. Nydia, who had overheard all, crept to the door that had closed upon Calenus.

Priest, unknown to Arbaces I have been a witness to his perfidy. If I myself can escape from these walls, I may save thee.

Did I hear aright? Canst thou save the Athenian Glaucus from the charge against his life?

Only free me, and he is safe. I saw Arbaces strike the blow. I can convict the true murderer. Revenge on the false Egyptian. Revenge!

Be cautious, sweet stranger. Seek the praetor, obtain his writ of search. Bring soldiers and smiths of cunning –– these locks are wondrous strong. Time flies. I may starve if you are not quick.

Nydia glided away until she found the mouth of the passage that led to the upper air. But there she paused.

It will be safer to wait until the night is so blended with the morning that the whole house will be buried in sleep.

While Nydia thus waited, Arbaces went to see Ione. But she drove him from her with scorn.

I will yet triumph over this woman.

As his attendants assisted him to unrobe for the night, the thought of Nydia flashed across him. Ione must never learn of Glaucus' frenzy, lest it excuse his crime.

Go to Sosia and tell him on no pretence is he to suffer the blind slave Nydia out of her chamber.

The freedman hastened to obey. He found Sosia, who told him of Nydia's escape.

Are you sure she has left the house? She may be hiding here yet.

How is that possible? She could have easily gained the garden, and the gate was open.

Nay, not so. I was lately in the garden and, seeing it open, closed and locked it.

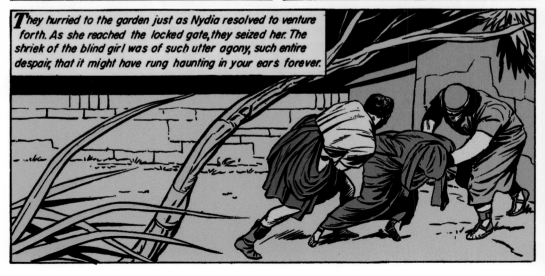

They hurried to the garden just as Nydia resolved to venture forth. As she reached the locked gate, they seized her. The shriek of the blind girl was of such utter agony, such entire despair, that it might have rung haunting in your ears forever.

It was now late on the last day of the trial of Glaucus. He had been found guilty. Meanwhile, the hours passed in lingering torture over the head of Nydia, who had been returned to her cell.

Sosia is my only hope. He wants his freedom. Am I not rich enough to purchase it? I have these bracelets and this chain.

She shrieked aloud and beat herself against the door. Sosia hastened to see what was the matter.

Kind Sosia, I cannot endure to be so long alone. Sit with me, I pray.

Mind, no tricks.

No, no, dear Sosia. Tell me, how much dost thou require to make up the purchase of thy freedom?

Why, about two thousand sestertia.

Seest thou these bracelets and this chain? They are well worth double that sum. I will give them thee if thou wilt only take a letter for me.

Give me the trinkets, and I will take the letter.

Nydia wrote upon a wax tablet and directed Sosia to take it to Glaucus' friend, Sallust. Sallust, however, was drinking to distract his grief over Glaucus.

I bring this from a young female.

A curse on these wenches.

He threw the letter on the table and was borne off to bed. The next morning, people poured rapidly into the city clad in holiday attire to see the gladiators and the criminals in the amphitheatre. Arbaces watched them.

Brutes! Are ye less homicides than I am? I slay but in self-defence — — ye make murder a pastime.

He called his slaves and went to the amphitheatre, which was quickly being filled by the impatient crowd.

All was ready. Now, with a loud and warlike flourish of trumpets, eight gladiators entered the arena.

How beautiful! But when will the lion eat Glaucus?

That is reserved for last.

The combatants were arranged in pairs, and the grave sports of the day commenced. The two horsemen were at either extremity of the lists and, at a given signal, started simultaneously.

One pierced the other through the breast. He reeled and fell.

The body of the loser was dragged away, and there were now six combatants in the arena. Two, each armed with a heavy Greek cestus*, advanced to the middle and commenced hostilities.

* leather thongs, loaded with lead or iron, wound around arms and hands

They struck at each other with hammerlike hands.

That blow would have crushed an ox!

Officers dragged off the stunned and insensible gladiator. There were now four combatants. One, a retiarius, or netter, was matched with a swordsman. The retiarius cast his net, but a quick inflection of the other gladiator's body saved him.

The retiarius now fled with the swordsman in hot pursuit as the people laughed and shouted.

Their attention was then turned to the two Roman combatants, who were in heated and fierce encounter. Soon the sword of one had inflicted the death wound upon the other.

Meanwhile, the retiarius had again cast his net, this time successfully. The gladiator struggled against its meshes in vain as the trident descended.

His body was dragged at once from the arena. A deep and breathless hush lay, like a mighty and awful dream, over the assembly.

Bring forth the lion and Glaucus, the Athenian.

Glaucus was led into the arena. The gaze of the spectators turned to the den of the lion.

The sign was given, the keeper cautiously removed the grating, and the lion leaped forth with a mighty and glad roar of release.

Glaucus stood ready, but to the astonishment of all, the beast seemed not even aware of his presence. Instead, it circled round and round the arena as if seeking only some avenue of escape.

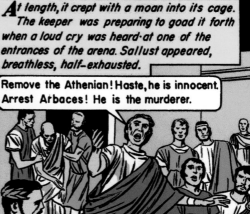

At length, it crept with a moan into its cage. The keeper was preparing to goad it forth when a loud cry was heard at one of the entrances of the arena. Sallust appeared, breathless, half-exhausted.

Remove the Athenian! Haste, he is innocent. Arrest Arbaces! He is the murderer.

The praetor rose from his seat.

Art thou mad, O Sallust!

Remove the Athenian! I bring with me the eyewitness to the death of Apaecides.

Pale, haggard, Calenus was supported into the very row in which Arbaces sat.

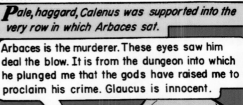

Arbaces is the murderer. These eyes saw him deal the blow. It is from the dungeon into which he plunged me that the gods have raised me to proclaim his crime. Glaucus is innocent.

The praetor gave orders for Glaucus to be removed under guard.

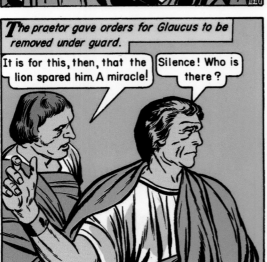

It is for this, then, that the lion spared him. A miracle!

Silence! Who is there?

Sallust led Nydia forward.

The blind girl Nydia. It is her hand that raised Calenus from the grave and delivered Glaucus from the lion.

The crowd, rendered savage by the exhibition of blood in the arena, now thirsted for more. A cry sprang up.

To the lion with the Egyptian!

The crowd poured down upon Arbaces who, looking up, beheld an awful apparition. He stretched his hand on high.

Behold! The fires burst forth against my accusers!

The eyes of the crowd followed the gesture of the Egyptian and beheld a vast vapour shooting from the summit of Vesuvius.

There was a dead silence. Then there arose the shrieks of women; the men stared at each other. At that moment they felt the earth shake beneath their feet and heard in the distance the crash of falling roofs.

An instant more and the mountain cloud seemed to roll toward them, dark and rapid; at the same time it cast forth a shower of ashes mixed with fragments of burning stone. The crowd turned to fly-- dashing, pressing, crushing against each other.

Meanwhile, Nydia had found her way to the small room to which Glaucus had been led and had flung herself at his feet.

It is I who saved thee. Now let me die!

Nydia, my child! My preserver!

They were interrupted by the cries of terrified people.

The mountain! The earthquake!

All fled, leaving Glaucus and Nydia to save themselves as they might. Upon learning that Ione was yet in the house of Arbaces, Glaucus took Nydia by the hand and hurried thither.

The darkness increased so rapidly that Glaucus could guide his steps only with difficulty. The columns of the house seemed to reel and tremble. Leaving Nydia without, he ascended to the upper rooms.

Ione! Ione!

At length, he heard her voice in reply. To rush forward, to shatter the door, to seize Ione in his arms, to hurry from the mansion, seemed to him the work of an instant.

They hastened onward, those three. Alas, whither? They now saw not a step before them -- the blackness became utter.

Amidst the other horrors, the mighty mountain now cast up columns of boiling water. The streams fell like seething mud over the streets.

As the blackness gathered, the lightnings around Vesuvius increased in their vivid and scorching glare. Sometimes the larger stones which fell broke into fragments, emitting sparks which caught whatever was combustible within their reach. Frequently, by this momentary light, parties of fugitives encountered each other.

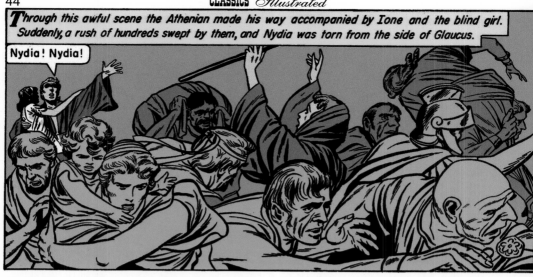

Through this awful scene the Athenian made his way accompanied by Ione and the blind girl. Suddenly, a rush of hundreds swept by them, and Nydia was torn from the side of Glaucus.

Nydia! Nydia!

Glaucus and Ione retraced their steps -- in vain. Their friend was lost.

How will we get to the sea now? Nydia, alone, knew her way in the dark.

They continued their uncertain way amid rushing winds that bore sharp streams of burning dust and poisonous vapours.

Oh, Glaucus. Take me to thy arms! One embrace, then let me die.

Courage yet, sweet Ione. See, torches come this way.

The torches flashed on Glaucus and Ione. Several slaves bore coffers heavily laden. In front of them towered the lofty form of Arbaces.

Fate smiles upon me even through these horrors. Away, Greek! I claim my ward, Ione.

Touch but the hand of Ione, and I will tear thee limb from limb!

Arbaces advanced one step. The ground shook beneath him. Lightning touched a tall column which rose behind him. Down it fell, crushing the great Arbaces.

Glaucus and Ione fled along the street. An avalanche of fire rushed down the mountain and forced them beneath the cover of an arch. It was there that Nydia found them.

Ah! Thou art safe!

Follow me! Take my hand!

Half-leading, half-carrying Ione, Glaucus followed his guide toward the shore. There they joined a group and put forth to sea.

Utterly exhausted, Ione slept on the breast of Glaucus, and Nydia lay at his feet. At last, softly, beautifully, the light dawned over the sea and the ruined city. Nydia rose gently. She bent over the sleeping Glaucus and kissed his brow.

She turned away, crept to the further side of the vessel and bent low over the deep.

I cannot endure it. This love shatters my whole soul. I have saved him. Why not die happy?

A sailor, half-dozing on the deck, heard a slight splash on the waters. He fancied he saw something white above the waves, but it vanished in an instant. When the lovers awoke, they searched for Nydia. But the blind Thessalian had vanished forever from the living world.

The End

Edward Bulwer-Lytton (1803-1873)

Edward Bulwer-Lytton was born Edward Bulwer in London, England, on May 25th, 1803. His family was well-to-do, but his father died when young Edward was four. Edward was very bright, and considered a prodigy, but his early education was somewhat haphazard. When he graduated from Cambridge in 1826, he had the reputation of a fashionable young man who was clever at fencing, boxing and playing a card game called whist.

He did not think of making literature his career until he married in 1827. Then his mother, disapproving of the match, cut off his allowance. Forced to earn a living, Bulwer turned to writing. In 1828, his second novel, *Pelham*, was a success. People who read it enjoyed trying to guess who Bulwer used as models for the characters in his book. After that, his books were very popular.

In 1831, he became a member of Parliament, where he served for twenty-four years. He also began to edit a magazine called the *New Monthly*, through which he met Charles Dickens and Benjamin Disraeli, who later became Prime Minister of England.

When Bulwer published *The Last Days of Pompeii* in 1834, excavations of the buried Roman city near Naples had been underway for about eighty-five years. After the eruption of Vesuvius in 79 A.D., in which two thousand people were killed, Pompeii was covered by twenty to thirty feet of cinders, ashes and lava deposits. Only the tops of the tallest buildings could be seen. Later eruptions of the volcano covered all trace of the city, and its remains stood in obscurity for nearly seventeen hundred years.

In the sixteenth century, an Italian architect discovered part of the ruins while excavating for an underground waterway, but it was not until 1748 that work on excavating the city was begun. From 1806 to 1814, during the French occupation of Italy, large parts of Pompeii were unearthed. In the city there stood a small temple of Isis, the only one of its kind to survive intact to modern times. Excavations in Pompeii are still going on. *The Last Days of Pompeii* was immediately popular. It and *Rienzi* are the only two of Bulwer's many novels that are still read today.

Bulwer was also successful as a playwright. The saying, "The pen is mightier than the sword," is a line from his play *Richelieu*, which he wrote in 1838.

When his mother died in 1843, Bulwer inherited her estate and added her maiden name, Lytton, to his own, becoming Edward Bulwer-Lytton. Because of his activity in Parliament, he received the post of colonial secretary in 1858. But in 1866, he was entitled Baron Lytton, which granted him a seat in the House of Lords, and he retired from politics.

Literary careers ran in the Bulwer family. Bulwer-Lytton's brother, Sir Henry Bulwer was the author of several historical and biographical works. Bulwer-Lytton's son, Edward Robert Bulwer, was a poet.

Edward Bulwer-Lytton died on June 18th, 1873, at the age of 70.

The Eruption of Mount Vesuvius

Pompeii was a thriving Roman city on the west coast of Italy and today its ruins lie within the City area of Napoli (Naples). Pompeii was founded around the 7th-6th century B.C. by the Osci or Oscans, a people of central Italy, on what was an important crossroad between Cumae, Nola and Stabiae. Pompeii was also captured by the Etruscans, and recent excavations have shown the presence of Etruscan inscriptions and a 6th century B.C. necropolis. It became a Roman colony called Colonia Cornelia Veneria Pompeianorum. The town became an important passage for goods that arrived by sea and had to be sent toward Rome or Southern Italy along the nearby Appian Way. Agriculture, water and wine production were also important.

It was fed with water by a spur from Aqua Augusta (Naples) built circa 20 B.C. by Agrippa; the main line supplied several other large towns, as well as the naval base at Misenum. By the 1st century A.D., Pompeii was one of a number of towns located around the base of the volcano, Mount Vesuvius. The area had a substantial population which had grown prosperous from the region's agricultural fertility. On August 24th, 79 A.D. Mount Vesuvius erupted, spewing tons of molten ash, pumice and sulphuric gas miles into the atmosphere. A "firestorm" of poisonous vapours and molten debris engulfed the surrounding area, suffocating the inhabitants of Pompeii, and the nearby towns of Herculaneum and Stabiae. Tons of falling debris filled the streets until nothing remained to be seen of the once thriving communities. The eruption was preceded by a powerful earthquake seventeen years beforehand on 5th February, A.D. 62, which caused widespread destruction around the Bay of Naples, and particularly to Pompeii. Some of the damage had still not been repaired when the volcano erupted. Another smaller earthquake took place in 64 A.D.; it was recorded by Suetonius in his biography of Nero and by Tacitus in Annales because it took place while Nero was in Naples performing for the first time in a public theatre. Suetonius recorded that the emperor continued singing through the earthquake until he had finished his song, while Tacitus wrote that the theatre collapsed shortly after being evacuated.

The eruption lasted two days. The morning of the first day was perceived as normal by the only eyewitness to leave a surviving document, Pliny the Younger. In the middle of the day an explosion threw up a high-altitude column from which ash began to fall, blanketing the area. Rescues and escapes occurred during this time. At some time in the night or early the next day pyroclastic flows in the close vicinity of the volcano began. Lights were seen on the mountain interpreted as fires. Persons as far away as Misenum fled for their lives. The flows were rapid-moving, dense and very hot, knocking down wholly or partly all structures in their path, incinerating or suffocating all population remaining there and altering the landscape, including the coastline. These were accompanied by additional light tremors and a mild tsunami in the Bay of Naples. By evening of the second day the eruption was over, leaving only haze in the atmosphere through which the sun shone weakly. It is not

Cont'd

known how many people the eruption killed. By 2003 around 1,044 casts made from impressions of bodies in the ash deposits had been recovered in and around Pompeii, with the scattered bones of another 100. The remains of about 332 bodies have been found at Herculaneum. What percentage these numbers are of the total dead or the percentage of the dead to the total number at risk remain completely unknown. By coincidence, the eruption occurred the day after Vulcanalia, the festival of the Roman god of fire.

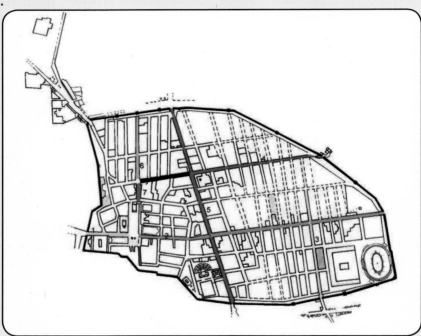

A Map of Pompeii, featuring the main roads, the Cardo Maximus is in Red and the Decumani Maximi are in green and dark blue. The southwest corner features the main forum and is the oldest part of the town.

Computer-generated imagery of the eruption of Vesuvius from BBC/Discovery Channel's co-production *Pompeii*.

Pompeii today, with Vesuvius in the distance.